Count Snobula Vamps It Up

Make way for the monsters from
MONSTER MANOR

MONSTER MANOR

Count Snobula Vamps It Up

by **PAUL MARTIN** and **MANU BOISTEAU**
Adapted by **LISA PAPADEMETRIOU**
Illustrated by **MANU BOISTEAU**

Hyperion Books for Children
New York

visit us at www.abdopublishing.com

Reinforced library bound edition published in 2012 by Spotlight, a division of ABDO Publishing Group, 8000 West 78th Street, Edina, Minnesota 55439. Spotlight produces high-quality reinforced library bound editions for schools and libraries. This edition reprinted by arrangement with Disney Book Group, LLC.

Printed in the United States of America, Melrose Park, Illinois.

052011

092011

 This book contains at least 10% recycled materials.

First published under the title *Maudit Manoir, Le Talisman de Dracunaze* in France by Bayard Jeunesse. © Bayard Editions Jeunesse, 2002 Text copyright © 2002 by Paul Martin Illustrations copyright © 2002 by Manu Boisteau Monster Manor and the Volo colophon are trademarks of Disney Enterprises, Inc. Volo® is a registered trademark of Disney Enterprises, Inc. Volo/Hyperion Books for Children are imprints of Disney Children's Book Group, L.L.C.

Library of Congress Cataloging-in-Publication Data
This title was previously cataloged with the following information:

Martin, Paul, 1968-
Count Snobula vamps it up / by Paul Martin and Manu Boisteau ; adapted by Lisa Papademetriou ; illustrated by Manu Boisteau.
p. cm. -- (Monster Manor ; #6)
Summary: Count Snobula gets no respect! When he finds out about a mysterious charm that has the power to change his luck, he is sure all of his problems are solved. Things start to go monstrously out of control when he asks his cousin for help. Count Snobula is about to find out that two vampires are one too many!
[1. Monsters --Fiction.]
I. Boisteau, Manu. II. Papademetriou, Lisa. III. Title. IV. Series.
PZ7.M3641833 Cou 2003
[FIC]--dc22
                        2005295536
ISBN 978-1-59961-887-6 (reinforced library bound edition)

All Spotlight books are reinforced library bindings and manufactured in the United States of America.

Contents

_I_f you're ever in Transylvaniaville, be sure to stop by Mon Staire Manor. Everyone calls it _Monster_ Manor... that's because a bunch of monsters live there.

The Haunted Hills

Nerdburg

Transylvaniaville

Malibu Nightclub

MALIBU

A Scary-looking Tree

The Slippen Falls

There are lots of fun things to do at the Manor. You can stroll through the cemetery, watch the swamp glow under the moonlight, or make a few new friends!

The FEMUR Family

EYE-GORE & STEVE

This sweet little family may look scary, but the truth is that they have no guts at all.

They want to be skate punks, but they're really just zombies with bad attitudes.

BEATRICE
Mon Staire

Wolf Man
STU

COUNT
SNOBULA

She's haunted by a horrible
secret... and a hairdo
that's even worse.

When the moon is full,
he becomes human.
Well, *somewhat* human...

He isn't rich, but he *is*
totally stuck up. Thank
goodness he sleeps all day.

Step through the gate—
let's see who's home!

The SWAMP HORROR

SALLY the Specter

Professor VON SKALPEL

It ain't easy being a big green ball of toxic slime!

Beatrice's mother is smart, sassy—and a ghost!

The most brilliant mad scientist in town. He's a real cutup.

FRANKIE

Created by Von Skalpel,
Frankie is one of a kind.
Thank goodness.

Take a look inside the Manor.
It might be old, but the monsters
think of it as "home, sweet home."

Von Skalpel's
Room

The Very Dark
Secret Room

Von Ska
Labora

The
Femur Crypt

Eye-Gore
and
Steve's Pit

The Radioactive Swamp

If you dare come inside, beware! Count Snobula the vampire will make you watch the finale of his favorite show, "Questions for a Champion," with him.

CHAPTER ONE
It's All Fun and Games

"*G*ive *me* the eyeball!" Wolf Man Stu shouted.

Steve, one of the zombies who lived in the cemetery behind Mon Staire Manor, reached for the marble eye but was stopped by the touch of a small, skeleton hand on his wrist.

"No way," Bonehead Femur replied, shaking his skull. "Thtu alwayth getth to be the eyeball," he lisped. "I want to be the eye for a change. Thtu, you can have the alien."

The wolf man bared his fangs and growled.

"Don't you understand that I'm a fearsome creature of the night? I could bury you in the backyard like a dog with a bone!"

"Oh, puh-leethe," Bonehead said. "Like I don't get buried every day." He had a good point—the little skeleton lived in the cemetery with the rest of his family. They had a comfortable crypt near the zombies' pit.

Steve handed the alien to the wolf man.

Outside the Manor, it was a cold December night. The villagers of Transylvaniaville were huddled in their homes, eating bowls of hot soup and blowing on mugs of hot chocolate. They called the manor Monster Manor because they thought a bunch of monsters lived there. If you had asked them what they thought the residents of the Manor were doing, they would no doubt have come up with some frightening theories—perhaps the creatures were creating a new monster, or snacking on a villager, or thinking of ways to attack the town.

But the villagers would have been dead wrong.

At that moment, everyone in Monster Manor was gathered in the living room around a large Monstrosity board. The creatures—and the humans—who lived in the Manor loved to play Monstrosity.

"I want the top hat," Count Snobula said.

Eye-Gore, Steve's brother, rolled his eyes so hard that one of them popped out of its socket. "Dude, there's no top hat. You can be a dragon, a vulture, an insane-looking wizard, something that looks like a heart, or a set of sharp teeth."

"Oooh! Teeth!" Count Snobula cried. He was a vampire, and proud of it. He grabbed the small set of sharp teeth and sniffed them.

"These smell lucky!"

"Um, I think that's mold," Frankie admitted. "I accidentally stored the box over one of the professor's boiling beakers." Frankie was a monster that the mad scientist, Professor Von Skalpel, had stitched together out of body parts he had dug up from the cemetery. Frankie assisted the professor with a lot of his experiments.

"I vill be zee vizard," Professor Von Skalpel said. He had a weird accent. He claimed to be from New Jersey, but nobody believed him.

"What about you, Horror?" Steve asked as he handed the wizard piece to the professor.

"Um, is there a jellyfish?" the Swamp Horror asked. Horror lived in the nearby swamp. He was large, green, and slimy. . . . But he was a really nice guy.

"Dude, we play this game *every* week," Eye-Gore griped. "Learn the pieces!"

"If I take the heart, can I pretend it's a jellyfish?" Horror asked.

"Oh, for crying out loud," snapped Beatrice Mon Staire. She picked up the piece and handed it to him. "Take it. It's a jellyfish. Can we get on with it?" Beatrice was the owner of the Manor, and a real witch. Actually, she couldn't really do much magic . . . but she was kind of witchy, sometimes.

After another three hours of arguing over who would get which pieces, the creatures finally started the game. The object was to win a kingdom full of treasure, and fake money was already piling up in front of Count Snobula, Steve, Professor Von Skalpel, and, especially, Bonehead. Beatrice had lost all of her money by overspending in order to build cheap shacks on her kingdom's land. Frankie kept moving his piece in the wrong direction, so the others finally made him quit. And Horror was terrible with money.

Wolf Man Stu rolled the dice. He only had three bills. "Seven," Stu said. He moved his alien game piece forward. "Risk," he read, eyeing the word written in the space. That meant he had to draw a card from the Risk pile. These cards tended to be either very lucky, or very, very unlucky. Stu picked up the card and read aloud: "A spaceship destroys your kingdom. Give the bank a million, billion, zillion dollars and leave the room." Stu growled and slapped the card onto the table.

Count Snobula cackled with glee. "Now the game is getting interesting," the vampire said. "Might I suggest a little wager?"

"What?" Bonehead said. "A wafer? Like, crackerth?"

"No, no, a *wager*," Snobula repeated. "A

bet. Winner takes all. I have a glow-in-the-dark pen I could throw in."

"I have a few kidneys I vill not be needing," the professor said.

"Hmmm . . ." Horror thought for a moment. "I've got some green Jell-O."

"I have a head of garlic," Bonehead said.

Snobula's face turned even paler than usual.

"Now, Bonehead, you know that's not funny," Tibia Femur, Bonehead's mother, warned. "Vampires hate garlic. Bet a skull—our crypt is full of them."

Bonehead giggled. "Okay. One thkull."

Count Snobula looked down at his kingdom and grinned. He had slightly more money and many more shacks on his properties than any of the others—except for Bonehead. This game—not to mention the kidneys, Jell-O, and skull—was his.

Snobula rolled the dice and moved his piece forward four spaces. "Collect three hundred dollars from every player," he read, from the square on which he'd landed.

The others groaned loudly as they handed over their money.

"Ha-ha!" Snobula cried. "And I get to roll again—I had doubles." This time, Snobula moved forward five spaces and landed on a Risk square. He picked up a card. *Your kingdom is plagued by giant, man-eating rats. One of them finds you and has a tasty snack. Hand over your fortune, and get lost!* it read. "Drat it all!" Snobula shouted. "And I was so close!"

He threw down his card and stalked off. "If anyone needs me, I'll be in my room," he said in a huff, but the creatures weren't listening. They had already moved on to the next roll.

CHAPTER TWO
Crypt-o-Night

Count Snobula pulled down the cover on his coffin and lay in the dark, thinking, Why do I always get sucked into betting? I should have listened to my grandmother.

Many years before, a young Vladu Snobula (now known as Count Snobula) had grown up in a palace with his grandmother, Ambrosia Snobula. Ambrosia had always warned Vladu about games of chance, and told him never to bet on anything. Naturally, that had made

Vladu want to bet on *everything*, and that is what he had proceeded to do.

He had bet his friends that it would rain the next day. He had bet his teachers that he would get an A on his next test. He had bet that he could hold his breath while someone else counted to infinity. He had bet and bet and bet until Ambrosia asked him why he no longer had shoes, or a backpack, or lunch, and why he had to go over to Kelly Finklestein's house to do her family's dishes for a month. Vladu Snobula had confessed the truth, and his grandmother had forbade him to bet ever again. And that had worked. Until he grew up and moved out of the castle, that is.

Once Vladu was on his own, he had inherited a large amount of money and started to call himself *Count* Snobula. He had bought a nice castle and had it redecorated. But once that was done, Count Snobula had discovered that he was bored, so he'd started spending his nights at the casino in town.

It had only taken him two weeks to lose everything but a small suitcase and the clothes on his back.

So the count had hit the road and finally arrived in Transylvaniaville. He had charmed Beatrice Mon Staire's mother, Sally—who had not yet become a ghost. Sally had thought the count was a classy guy, so she had let him live in the shabby vault at the bottom of the stairs.

Not that I like this stupid vault, Count Snobula thought as he lay in his coffin. *I want to live in a palace again!*

Just as the count really started to get worked up, there was a knock at the door.

"Who is it?" Snobula called. He had to shout to be heard through his coffin.

"It'th Bonehead. I won the game—I've come for my glow-in-the-dark pen!"

Grumbling, Snobula threw open the top of his coffin. "Just a minute!" he shouted. "I have to put some things away—so that they won't frighten you!" Snobula kicked a stiff pair of socks behind a gargoyle. He swung open the door. "Come in," he said.

"Wow, neat crypt," the little skeleton said

as he walked inside the vampire's room.

"Thank you," Snobula replied. "I like to think that I'm not such a bad crypt-keeper. Now, let me see." He peered up at the highest shelf in his closet, where a leather suitcase sat, covered in a layer of dust. Snobula pulled it down, and dust flew everywhere.

"Cool!" Bonehead cried. "It'th like fog!"

Snobula choked. "Er . . . yes. I keep it dusty on purpose."

Snobula flipped open the lid and peered inside. He hadn't looked inside the suitcase since he had left his grandmother's palace, but he was pretty sure that his old pen was still in there. "Drat! Where is that thing?" Snobula cried, feeling

around beneath his baby blanket. Suddenly, his hand closed around something metal. He pulled it out and saw that it was a small, locked chest. Attached to the top of the chest there was an envelope with a red ribbon tied in a bow.

"What ith it?" Bonehead asked.

"I don't know," Snobula replied. Suddenly, he remembered that the pen was tucked into a small corner pocket of the bag. He dug it out and handed it to Bonehead.

"Awethome!" the little skeleton said and hurried off.

Count Snobula sighed. He'd had that pen since he had been a young vampire, and he hated to lose it. But there was nothing he could do about it now. He turned his attention back to the chest. He didn't remember packing it—what could be in it? He untied the decaying envelope and pulled out the letter inside.

My dear, beloved Vladu,

You are leaving the castle, and I will soon find my way to the family crypt for a nice, long nap. I'm slipping this message into your suitcase, because I want to keep it a secret between us.

Inside this chest is a lucky charm. It could change the course of everything, and I want to be sure that it goes to the right person. I know that you like to make bets, my dear, and this could make all of your dreams come true if you take the right risk.

Your cousin, Odette, who now lives in Texas, is my only other grandchild. I've given the chest to you, but I gave the combination to the lock to her. She should have no trouble remembering it.

Once destiny brings you two together, you'll have the power to unlock the chest. The good-luck charm must go to whoever will carry on the Snobula name with the greatest splendor. I know that you will choose wisely.

With a big kiss,

Grandma Ambrosia

P.S. I mended your black scarf and put it in the bottom of this suitcase. Don't catch a cold!

Count Snobula couldn't believe that it had been so long since he had opened that suitcase.

So many years wasted! I could have been rich! I could have moved out years ago, Snobula thought. With a lucky charm, I could have gone to Las Vegas and hit the jackpot.

But it wasn't too late!

The count reached into the bottom of the bag and pulled out the black scarf. He wrapped it around his neck and grinned. Much better.

And now . . . on to my fortune, he thought with a grin.

CHAPTER THREE
Boxing

"Heh-heh-heh." Count Snobula chuckled as he reviewed his plan. "It's both simple and brilliant," the count said to himself as he rubbed his hands together greedily.

Part one: Open the chest without telling Cousin Odette.

Part two: Become rich.

Really, everything hinged on Part one.

Snobula frowned at the box. He yanked at the lock, but it wouldn't budge. It was made of thick, strong metal, and it required a six-digit combination to open. Hmmm . . . Count Snobula thought. I wonder if I can guess the combination?

Count Snobula put in his birth date—but that wasn't it. He tried his baby weight. Then he tried his grandmother's birthday; the day she purchased her favorite man-eating bougain-villea vine; the date of her wedding to Count Snobula's grandfather, Volker; the date of the time she had won ten dollars in the lottery; the birth date of Smoopsie-Poo—her beloved three-toed sloth, and the date of his own parents' dis-appearance. But none of those were it, either.

The count pounded on the chest with his fists in frustration. "Open!" he shouted.

The lock didn't budge.

In a rage, Snobula rooted through his coffin, finally finding a hammer. He pounded the box several times with the hammer, but that didn't even make the slightest dent.

Either this is one really strong box, Count Snobula thought, or I need to start getting to the gym more.

What I need is some brute force, the count decided. Which gives me an idea . . .

"Go avay!" Professor Von Skalpel shouted when he heard the polite tap at his laboratory door. "I am vorking!"

Ignoring him, Count Snobula swung open the door and gave the professor his cheeriest smile—which looked like a horrible grimace of pain, to tell you the truth (the old vampire didn't do a lot of smiling). "Hello, professor!" Snobula chirped, trying to be friendly. "Working hard, are we?"

"I'm vorking on a trooss zerum," Professor

Von Skalpel said in a huff. "I am tired of everyvun cheating at Monschtroschity. I'm zick of all you liars!"

"What a wonderful idea!" the count said, lying through his long, pointy teeth. He got right down to business. "Could I borrow a sledgehammer, a chisel, and Frankie?"

Professor Von Skalpel rubbed his beard, thinking it over. "Vell, okay. Just be careful."

"Oh, I'll take good care of Frankie," Snobula promised.

"Not him—be careful viz zee sledgehammer!" Von Skalpel replied. "Zose sings are expensive!"

"Frankie, I lost my key to this box," Count Snobula said a few moments later, as he and Frankie stood in his crypt. Frankie was holding the sledgehammer, which was normally

used for breaking up boulders. "Do you think you could open it for me without crushing whatever—I mean, my very important, uh, *thing*—inside?"

Frankie frowned. "What's inside?"

Count Snobula tried to think of something. "Uh . . . my toothbrush. I put it in there so it wouldn't get dirty."

Frankie placed the chisel on the lock. He raised the sledgehammer high over his head. Then, with a mighty heave, he brought the hammer down with all of his strength.

Monster Manor shook with the power of

Frankie's heavy blow.

But when Snobula ran to the box to grab his good-luck charm, he discovered that the metal box was unharmed. It didn't have a scratch.

"What's this?" the count cried. "The box is perfectly fine!"

"That makes one of us," Frankie said woozily. The force of his blow had been so powerful that the stitches holding his right

arm in place had come undone. His arm fell to the floor with a sad *thunk*!

Count Snobula sighed. "Well," he said slowly, "at least the sledgehammer is okay."

"Er . . . professor?" Snobula said carefully as he knocked lightly on the laboratory door. He just hoped that Von Skalpel was in a good mood and wouldn't be too angry about Frankie's arm.

"Snobula!" the professor shouted.

"I'm so sorry about Frankie. . . ." Snobula said.

"Vhat?" the professor asked. "Vhat are you talking about? Come in, come in. I vant to show you somesing. Look!" He pointed to a cage of large rats.

"Uh, I gotta be honest with you, pal," one of the rats said to the professor, "you're getting a little bit bald on top."

"That's amazing!" Count Snobula whispered, gaping at the rat.

"I know!" the professor replied. "My trooss zerum is vorking! Zee zerum schpilled all over zee rats, and now zey tell zee trooss all zee time!" Professor Von Skalpel looked at the count expectantly. "So—vas Frankie helpful?"

"Um . . . I'm afraid he's a little damaged," the count admitted.

"Oh, zat is nozing," the professor said. "I

have a better arm in storage, anyvay. Von zat Frankie vill like much better."

"I couldn't even help the count open his chest," Frankie said sadly.

"Thanks, anyway," Snobula said. He'd just have to think of something else.

Back in his room, Snobula was spinning the numbers of the combination again. He'd decided that he needed a method, so he started with six zeroes, then moved on to 000001, 000002, 000003, and so on. "I'll get this combination eventually," Snobula muttered.

Snobula's eyes started to cross by the time he hit 000555, and by the time he was at 000879, he thought he was going to scream.

Once he reached 000999, he really did scream. "There are a million combinations!" he shouted, giving the box an angry kick.

All right, the count said to himself as he paced his small vault. I'd hoped that it wouldn't come to this, but it's time to move on to Plan B. Granny's letter said that the combination was something that Odette would easily remember. That must mean that it has something to do with her in particular. All I have to do is ask her a few questions. . . .

Count Snobula picked up a pen and began to write.

CHAPTER FOUR
More Than He Bargained For

"Is this banner really necessary, Mr. Mayor?" asked Wilhelm Z. Cleenup, the head janitor for City Hall. He was standing at the top of a ladder, holding up one end of a cloth sign that read WELCOME TO TRANSYLVANIAVILLE'S 57TH ANNUAL CHILI FEST! "I mean, Transylvaniaville isn't really known for its chili."

Oswald B. Smiley, the one and only mayor of Transylvaniaville, grinned broadly. "Not yet, Willie," he said. "But by the time I unleash the planned media blitz, the words *Transylvaniaville* and *chili* will be glued together in everyone's mind. Rich tourists will come from all over the world to try our very own special town recipe."

"What have you got planned for the media blitz?" Willie asked.

Mayor Smiley looked shocked. "You mean, you think we need to do *more* than hang this banner?"

At that moment, a sleek, black limousine with tinted windows cruised down Main Street. The car was almost as tall as it was wide, and bore a strange resemblance to a hearse. It moved so silently it seemed almost to glide over the pavement.

The car pulled to a stop and the window slid down. "Mon Staire Manor?" someone asked in a husky voice tinged with an accent of some kind or another. It was hard to place.

Mayor Smiley flashed a brilliant grin and rubbed his hands together. "Of course!" he said "Straight ahead, at the top of the hill."

The window was rolled up, and the car glided away.

The mayor was so excited that he gave a little hop. "Did you see the license plate, Willie?" he cried. "Texans! Oil-rich, Texan tourists, ready to eat chili and spend money! Gosh—why didn't I think of it before? This whole fes-

Not bad . . .

Personally, I prefer an SUV. . . .

tival needs to have a Western theme. I'm going to buy a ten-gallon hat right now!"

"But we aren't even in the west," Willie said.

"Who cares?" the mayor shouted. "It's all about the marketing!"

A large limousine glided into the Manor's driveway. The Manor didn't get many visitors, and when Count Snobula heard the sound of crunching gravel, he woke with a start. He ran to the top of the stairs and peeked out the window. A car with a Texas license plate—it couldn't be!

"Yoo-hoo!" cried out a woman's voice. "Anybody out there?"

Count Snobula hurried to the limousine and opened the rear door. But it was completely empty.

"In the back!" the voice screeched.

Snobula shut the door and jogged to the limo's trunk. He yanked it open and found a coffin inside. He threw the lid open, and a woman with enormous hair leaped out and wrapped Count Snobula in a huge hug.

"Vladdie!" the woman screeched. "You handsome devil! It's been ages!"

"Cousin Odette," Count Snobula said, trying to unwrap his cousin's arms from his neck. "What a surprise."

The moment Odette stepped out of the trunk, it closed behind her. Almost immediately, the car began to glide away.

"Bye-bye, Otto!" Odette called after the car. "He's my chauffeur," she explained. "He's invisible, but an excellent driver." She grinned, and the dimples in her cheeks showed. Cousin Odette certainly didn't look like a vampire. For one thing, she was slightly plump. For another, she wore a purple-velour tracksuit and sunglasses set with glittery, fake diamonds. "Hello, kiddies!" she called, waving to the Femur kids, Bonehead and his sister, Kneecap, who were hiding behind some bushes.

The Femurs giggled and ran away.

"Are those two your kids?" Odette asked Snobula. "They have your sickly complexion."

"No, no," the count said quickly. "Those are just my neighbors.

We're all monsters here."

"Holy cow!" Odette squealed as she turned and took in the front of the Manor. "Your place is gorgeous!"

Count Snobula blinked. His cousin thought that the Manor was his.

I should clear this up right now, Snobula thought. I should tell her the absolute truth. I *should*—but I won't.

"Yes, I bought the Manor and turned it into a monster bed-and-breakfast a few years ago," he said, lying.

"What a fabulous idea!" Odette cried. "I should do something like that with my ranch in Texas. It's big enough for it."

"So—Odette—what brings you to my humble abode?" Count Snobula asked. He couldn't wait another minute.

"You silly man!" Odette cried, punching

the count in the shoulder.

"Ha-ha!" The count winced and rubbed his shoulder. "That's me—so very, very silly."

"I'm here because of your sweet letter! I couldn't believe that you were so interested in all the details of my life—my birth date, the size of my underwear, my favorite lottery number! I decided that we'd been out of touch for too long. So I came for a visit. Now—I'd love to have a tour of the house, if you don't mind."

"Of course," Snobula said, grinning as widely as he could. "A tour."

He had to find a way to show Odette around without making her suspicious. . . . and without running into the other monsters. There was no doubt about it—this was going to be tricky.

CHAPTER FIVE
The Grand Tour

"Vladdie, this place is amazing!" Cousin Odette said as she stared at an enormous spiderweb stretched between two rusted suits of armor in the Manor's front hall. "It's so creepy—just like Grandma's house!"

Count Snobula chuckled. "I don't like to brag. . . ." he bragged, "but it cost a fortune. I hired a decorator from France who knows all about ancient castles and ruins."

Odette looked up at the ceiling and let out

a low whistle. "How much did it cost to make those cracks and peeling paint look so real?"

Snobula held up a hand. "You don't even want to know."

"What's this?" Odette asked, yanking open a large, metal door marked KEEP OUT! Before Snobula could stop her, she pranced into Professor Von Skalpel's laboratory.

"Who are you?" the professor asked, catching sight of Odette. He was holding out a beaker of bloodred liquid, and seemed momentarily dazzled by her large hair and rhinestone glasses.

"I'm Vladdie's cousin, Odette," she said, extending his hand. "Are you the butler?"

"Butler?" the professor repeated, frowning. "No—and who is Vladdie?"

But Odette wasn't paying attention to the professor anymore. She had been distracted by a green stain in the middle of the floor.

"Oh, that is just so cute!" Odette gushed. "This is supposed to look like a mad scientist's lab! How much was this crazy, stained tile, Vladdie? Oooh—and that beaker set—I have to have one! What's this?" Odette yanked the top off a jar, and a cloud of huge, mutant flies flew out. "Fabulous!" Odette cried.

"Vhat are you doing?" Von Skalpel cried. He was about to add, *Frankie, schtop zis voman!* but Count Snobula pressed his hand

over the professor's mouth and dragged him into a corner.

"Odette is my rich cousin," Snobula whispered in the professor's ear. "She's from Texas, and she's come here looking for interesting projects to donate money to. She is extremely interested in research. . . ."

The professor raised his eyebrows. "Vell, vhy didn't you zay zo? You know I have a number of different experiments zat look promising—"

Just then, Odette pulled the lid off a pot and peered inside. A purple tentacle wrapped itself around her neck and gave a yank.

"Frankie! Help zat voman!" the professor shouted.

Frankie ran over to the tentacle and poked at it with a fork until it let go. It took a moment for Odette's face to turn from blue to

pale green, but when it did, she said, "That was great! Very realistic!"

Snobula was starting to get a headache.

"Vladdie, I really think I should freshen up," Odette said. "Where's my room?"

The count cleared his throat. "I'd better help the professor clean up. Uh, Frankie," he said slowly, "won't you show my cousin to the best room in the house?"

"Certainly, Count Snobula," Frankie said. He used his newly fixed arm to pick Odette up and sling her over his shoulder.

Odette let out a giggle. "Oh, this is too much, Vladdie! Your staff is wonderful!"

Frankie trudged up the stairs to the finest room in the entire Manor—Beatrice's bedroom. "Here you go," he said as he plopped Odette down on the spiderweb bedspread.

"Thank you, dear," Odette said.

Odette turned toward the mirror that stood near Beatrice's bed. "Oh, my!" Odette said as she caught sight of her reflection. "A magic mirror! This is just amazing!"

Since vampires can't be seen in a normal mirror, it had been over three years since Odette had really been able to do her hair properly. She always had to go to the beauty salon. "My goodness—my hair is purple?" she squealed, looking at her reflection in the mirror.

"Might I say that that hair color looks ravishing on you," the mirror replied.

"Well, thank you," Odette said.

"Really, I think that the purple of your hair brings out the red of your eyes," the mirror went on. "It's a very good color for a vampire."

Odette giggled. "Mirror, mirror, on the stand, am I the fairest in the land?"

"Well . . ." the mirror hedged, "you're certainly the fairest in the *room*."

Just then, Beatrice kicked open the door.

"And now we have a tie," the mirror said.

"Mirror!" Beatrice barked, "I've told you before—never speak to strangers!"

"Oh, are you the maid?" Odette asked sweetly. "Because I'd really like some—"

"Maid?" Beatrice screeched. "I'm Beatrice Mon Staire. I own this Manor, and you're in my room! And you'd better get out before I turn you into a toilet-bowl brush!" This was, of course, an empty threat. Beatrice could barely turn a toilet-bowl brush into a toilet-bowl brush. But Odette didn't know that, and

so she let out a fairly loud shriek of terror, as Beatrice flapped her arms about dramatically.

"Beatrice!" Count Snobula shouted as he burst into the room. "Wait! I know this woman!"

Beatrice glared at the count. "What's she doing in my room?"

"This woman says that she owns the Manor," Odette wailed. "And she threatened to turn me into a toilet-bowl brush! She's crazy, Vladdie! Tell her—tell her that you're the owner."

Beatrice's eyebrows flew up.

Count Snobula cleared his throat. "Uh, well . . ." he sputtered, "the truth is . . . Beatrice is my wife! We both own the Manor!"

Beatrice's mouth fell open, but no sound came out.

"Vladdie! Congratulations—this is such

happy news!" Odette cried, grinning hugely. "I had no idea you were married."

"Darling!" Snobula said as he wrapped Beatrice in a warm hug. He drew her near and whispered, "Please play along; I'll explain everything."

"This had better be good, Snobula," she hissed.

"Oh, it will be. . . ." he promised.

As soon as I have a chance to make something up, he thought.

"Odette, why don't you take a stroll around the yard?"

Beatrice folded her arms across her chest as Odette left the room. "Well?" Beatrice demanded.

Count Snobula sighed. "It's a very sad story. Odette is madly in love with me, and has been for years. I had to tell her that I was married. It's only for a few days. Won't you help me?" Snobula pleaded.

Beatrice let out an exasperated sigh. "Oh, all right," she said, grudgingly. "But if she's not out of this Manor tomorrow, I'm throwing the both of you out!"

"Don't worry—I'll make sure she leaves," Snobula promised as he hurried out the door.

When I discover that secret code, he added silently.

CHAPTER SIX
Odette Goes Batty

As Count Snobula ran from the Manor, he heard a shout coming from the direction of the cemetery.

"What?" Steve's voice shouted. "Move? No way—not for ten million dollars!"

"But you wouldn't really even have to move!" Odette cried. "Only your crypt would be moving! You could stay in it!"

"What's going on here?" Count Snobula demanded as he strode into the cemetery.

Odette was sitting on a tomb next to the Femur family vault, surrounded by the skeletons. The zombies, Steve and Eye-Gore, were standing nearby, and they did not look happy. Fibula, the father and head of the Femur family, was excitedly punching numbers into a calculator.

"Cousin—I'm in love," Odette announced. "With this cemetery! It's just the thing for my ranch! How much do you want for it?"

Before the vampire could answer, Fibula waved the calculator at Odette. "Between the price of the land and the cost of taking apart our crypt, then moving it and putting it back together in Texas, I'll need at least two million, and that's just for our vault. You'll have to ask Beatrice about the rest."

"No problem!" Odette said quickly. "I'll have my lawyer draw up a contract."

"Would you like to come inside, so we can hammer out the details?" Fibula asked, beckoning toward his vault.

The count's eyes widened in horror. He couldn't let Odette buy the Femurs' vault—Beatrice would squash him! "Um . . . Odette, would you mind if I had a word with Mr. Femur in private?"

"No *problem-o*," Odette said casually.

"Fibula, I'm sorry to disappoint you,"

"Femur" with one M.

Count Snobula said quickly, once his cousin was out of earshot, "but that woman is completely nuts. She hasn't got a ranch in Texas, and she'll probably pay you in dryer lint."

"Wow," Fibula said, shaking his head slowly, "and she seemed so normal." He looked over to where Odette was lying on the ground, rolling around in the dirt. "I guess you never can tell. Come on, kids," he said, and the family disappeared into their vault.

The zombies trudged off too, glad that they wouldn't have to move to Texas. "Although I have always wanted to see a rodeo," Eye-Gore grumbled as he left.

Count Snobula trotted over to his cousin and helped her to her feet. "Odette, I need

to explain something to you. This cemetery has belonged to my landlady—I mean, my wife—and her family for centuries. Most of her ancestors are buried here, and some of them aren't even completely dead yet—"

"Oh," Odette said, her eyes wide. "I see. I'm sorry, Vladdie. I just found the cemetery so charming. . . ."

"We all do," Snobula assured her. "And you

can visit it here any time you like. Now," the count added brightly, taking Odette by the hand, "it's time for us to catch up."

He had to keep her talking. He needed that secret code!

"Yes," Count Snobula said, "you're my closest relative, but I don't even know the birth dates of any of your pets. . . ."

"Oh, Vladdie, can we talk about this later? I'm starving! Are there any villagers nearby? I need a snack!"

Count Snobula rolled his eyes. The last time he'd tried to catch one of the Transylvaniaville villagers, he had ended up with a pitchfork in the butt. Since then, he'd been hitting Professor Von Skalpel's frozen blood supply.

"Well . . ." Count Snobula hedged. ". . . It's just that the town is awfully far away. And the villagers are terrified of me, so they lock their doors and hang up garlic."

"Well, not tonight!" Odette said brightly. "They're having a festival. I'm sure they're all out and about—all we have to do is turn ourselves into bats and sneak into town."

Count Snobula grew even paler than usual. He hated turning into a bat. For one thing, it took a lot of practice, and it was harder than it sounded. And besides, it made his back hurt. But he didn't want Odette to know that—she'd think he was a pretty pathetic vampire.

"Okay," Count Snobula said slowly, "why don't you go pick out a nice, juicy villager? I'll meet up with you later. I'd better go tell my wife where I'm headed."

"Sounds great!" Odette said. She turned into a plump, black bat, and was flying off in the direction of the village.

Count Snobula hurried toward the Manor,

but he wasn't going to talk to his "wife," Beatrice. No—he was going to search through Odette's bags.

The secret had to be in there. And he had to find it!

CHAPTER SEVEN
A Dark and Chili Night

"Welcome, Transylvaniavillians and tourists!" Mayor Smiley said from the podium, announcing the opening of the Chili Festival.

The villagers looked around. There were only twenty people at the festival, and none of them were tourists. . . . unless the tourists were disguised as villagers.

The mayor continued. "Transylvaniaville chili is known throughout the world as the spiciest, meatiest, tastiest chili there is! The blend of herbs and spices—not to mention the secret ingredient—is what makes it so special. Let's hear it for our chili!"

The villagers cheered, spewing chunks of beef at the walls of the Malibu.

Hmmm . . . The mayor thought as he eyed the mess. Next time, I guess we should serve the chili *after* I give the speech.

Mayor Smiley stepped away from the podium just in time to see a plump woman in a velour tracksuit walk into the room. There could be no doubt—it was the Texan who had arrived in town earlier that day.

"Howdy!" Odette said brightly.

The villagers scowled at her. That was the way the folks in Transylvaniaville liked to greet strangers.

But Mayor Smiley knew that that wouldn't go over well with a Texan. He wanted to greet her personally. He emptied his bowl of chili, had a soda to wash the taste out of his mouth, and then strode forward to greet the visitor.

"Hi, there!" he said, giving Odette a wet and sloppy kiss on the hand. "I'm the mayor of Transylvaniaville."

"Charmed," Odette replied. "What a cute little town festival!"

"Thank you," Mayor Smiley replied. "But you don't have a bowl of chili! We have to get you one."

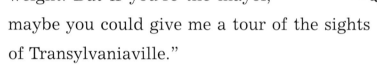

As we say when it's cold, "Hope you're not too chili!" Ha! Ha!

Odette wrinkled her nose. She was hungry—but not for chili. "Actually . . ." she said, "I'm watching my weight. But if you're the mayor, maybe you could give me a tour of the sights of Transylvaniaville."

"Well," the mayor said, checking his watch. "I guess I have the time."

Mayor Smiley and Odette stepped outside the dark village. Night had fallen, and two of the town's three streetlamps were broken, so Odette couldn't see much. Not that there was much to see.

"There's the post office," the mayor said, pointing to a squat building. "And there's the shoe store. And behind us is . . ."

The vampire smiled at the mayor,

and suddenly, Mayor Smiley found that he couldn't concentrate. He was hypnotized by the red flecks in Odette's eyes. She leaned forward.

"What is happening to me?" the mayor asked, woozily. He was so groggy that he put extra stress on the *h*'s, and his smelly breath wafted all over Odette.

"Aaaaarrrggghh!" Odette screamed. Then she shoved the mayor away.

Mayor Smiley was so groggy that he didn't even see it when the only tourist in town turned herself into a bat and flew away.

CHAPTER EIGHT
The Secret Ingredient!

"Let's see—fifteen," Count Snobula said as he spun the numbers on the combination lock. He was sitting on the moldy bed in the green room with the metal box in his lap and Odette's papers and clothing strewn around him. He'd already tried every date, phone number, and address listed in her organizer, and now he had moved on to trying her clothing sizes. "Okay, so it isn't her shoe size," the count said aloud as the lock refused to budge.

Snobula let out a big, exasperated sigh. "Maybe the code doesn't have anything to do with Odette's life, after all. I guess I'll just have to go back to trying every single combination. Let's see, where was I? Oh, yes: 00099—"

Just then, Odette flung open the door. "Vladdie!" she cried. Her eyes widened as she stared at her clothing and personal papers, which were strewn everywhere. "Thanks so much for unpacking for me! How sweet!"

"Er . . . you're welcome," the count said, as he tucked the chest into his cape.

Odette walked over and flopped onto the bed. "Oh, Vladdie, what a horrible night! I cornered a nice, fat villager—but he breathed

on me, and the smell . . ." She shuddered.

"Ah, yes," Snobula said, nodding, "the villagers have horrible breath."

"It was worse than that!" Odette insisted. "He reeked of garlic!"

"So that's the mystery ingredient in the chili!" Snobula cried.

Odette plumped up a pillow and leaned back. "What I wouldn't give for a nice glass of blood."

"Well . . . I might have some, down in the basement," Snobula admitted, thinking of the professor's stash in the lab. The vampire had an idea. He had seen Professor Von Skalpel's truth serum—it was bloodred. If he could find a way to feed the serum to Odette, she would have to tell him the combination.

"Oh, Vladdie, would you mind getting me some?" Odette asked sweetly.

"Not at all, cousin," Count Snobula said honestly. "I wouldn't mind one bit."

"Hello?" Count Snobula called as he swung open the laboratory door. "Anybody experimenting?"

There was no reply—the lab was deserted. Snobula peered among the many bottles, flasks, and beakers until he came to one that was bright red. "There you are!" he said to the

beaker. "The precious truth serum!"

He picked up the beaker, but, just as he turned around, he spotted another beaker—also filled with red liquid.

"Drat!" Snobula shouted. "Why does Professor Von Skalpel have to drink so much fruit punch?"

Snobula frowned at the beakers—one had to be truth serum, and the other, the professor's favorite drink. But how could he tell the difference?

"Vhat do you mean? I sought zat zee lady vas interested in my research!"

It was the professor's voice—and he was headed for the lab with the others. Quickly, the count hid behind a large barrel at the rear of the lab.

"I sought she vould give me two or sree million for my snot pump!"

"No, no, no," the count heard Fibula Femur insist. "I'm telling you, Snobula told me that she hasn't got a dime."

"But he told me that she was only here because she was madly in love with him!" Beatrice cried.

There was a moment of silence.

"And you believed it?" Fibula asked.

This lab is for experiments only!

"Okay, so he's obviously lying," Beatrice said.

"Zo—I have a zolution! My trooss zerum!" the scientist shouted.

The count panicked. Without thinking, he jumped into the barrel in front of him to hide. Unfortunately, it was filled with putrid old body parts, and made a horrible squishing sound as he dived in.

"Vhat vas zat?" the professor asked.

Snobula sighed. The jig was up.

CHAPTER NINE
The Jig Is Not Up

Count Snobula climbed out of the barrel, covered in sticky goo, and stepped out of the shadows.

"Snobula!" Von Skalpel cried. "Vhat happened?"

"It's my cousin!" Snobula pointed toward the storage closet. "She drank one of your experiments and—oh, the horror! Help her, please! She's in the closet!"

Von Skalpel, Beatrice, and Fibula hurried

into the coat closet to help.

"Wait a minute!" Beatrice cried. "There's no one in here!"

Count Snobula slammed the door shut and fastened the bolt. Ha-ha! Now he had a few hours to ask Odette the combination, open the box, and leave town with the good-luck charm!

"Count Snobula, are you all right?" asked a voice behind him.

Snobula turned and saw Frankie, who looked worried. "I heard shouting," Frankie explained. "You look terrible!" he added when he caught sight of the count's ruined clothing. "Like you just dived into a barrel of body parts!"

"No—I had a fight with a very slimy ghost," Snobula explained. "I've locked him in the broom closet, but I'm afraid he'll get out."

There was a loud, fierce banging from the other side of the door, and a muffled "Aaaaaaarrrrrnnnnggghhh!"

"I'll guard the door," Frankie said quickly. "I won't let him out, don't worry!"

Snobula grinned. This was perfect. And Frankie could help him with something else, too. . . . He pulled the two beakers of red liquid from his cape. "Thanks, Frankie," he said. "Here, have a sip of this. You need to keep up your strength!"

Frankie took a sip and licked his lips. Then his eyes seemed to glaze over.

"Who are you?" Snobula asked; he was checking to see if the truth serum worked.

"I amFrankie."

Good, good! Thank you, Frankie. If ever you're performing in town, don't forget to save me a ticket.

"Very good. What do you do?" the count went on.

"I am a famous singer," Frankie said.

Count Snobula frowned. "A singer?"

"Yes. My hit, 'Bit by the Werewolf of Love,' was number one for three months."

Actually, that was true. In his spare time, Frankie recorded pop songs in Professor Von Skalpel's secret recording studio, and many of them had gone double and even triple platinum. But Count Snobula only listened to classical music, and he had no idea about Frankie's hobby.

"Okay," the count said, staring at the beaker he had given to Frankie. "So, clearly, that's the fruit punch. Which is good, because I'm awfully thirsty."

And with that, Count Snobula gulped down the entire beaker—of truth serum.

CHAPTER TEN
Snobula Takes a Risk

"Yes, Odette—it's the truth," Count Snobula cried, "I've been trying to get the combination from you so that I could open the chest! I tried to cheat you out of the family fortune!"

Snobula had been jabbering away at his cousin for the past hour and a half. He had listed every sin he'd ever committed, from stealing a pack of gum from the corner store when he was six years old to replacing Odette's glass of blood with ketchup when they were twelve, and on and on, all the way up to losing his inheritance and trying to cheat her out of her fair share of the good-luck charm.

Odette took a swig of fruit punch and patted her cousin on the arm. "Oh, Vladdie," she said. "Is that the reason you wanted to know all about me?"

"Well—yes," Snobula admitted. "But I really have enjoyed seeing you again," he added. And, since he was still under the influence of the truth serum, Odette knew that he really meant it.

"Same here," Odette said. "As for the combination—it has nothing to do with me at all. It's just something that's easy to remember—"

Just then, footsteps pounded on the stairs, and a voice yelled, "Vere are zey?"

The bedroom door flew open, and Von Skalpel lurched inside, followed by Beatrice,

Fibula, and Frankie.

"Snobula!" the professor shrieked. "You locked us up, you told Frankie ve vere a slimy ghost—" Just then, the professor caught sight of the two empty beakers. "And you drank my fruit punch!"

"And your truth serum," Snobula added truthfully.

"And my trooss zerum, too? It just gets vorse and vorse!"

"Listen, darlings," Odette said quickly,

"Vladdie told me everything. He lied, it's true, but soon he'll have a good-luck charm, and he'll be rich and powerful again!"

Beatrice, Fibula, the professor, and Frankie stared at Odette for a minute in silence. They were totally confused.

"Vladdie! Open the window!"

"But it's cold outside," the count whined.

Odette lunged at the window and flung it wide open. Then she shoved Snobula out the window and jumped after him, laughing wildly.

Count Snobula panicked. The ground was coming at him pretty quickly. . . .

"Vladdie! Let's show them a thing or two!" Odette shouted. In a flash, she turned into a sleek, black bat and wheeled above Snobula's head.

Count Snobula groaned and flexed all of

Hang on, Vladdie! You're doing great!

his shriveled old muscles. His bones creaked, and his stomach lurched. Then, all of a sudden, he was transformed!

Okay, so he turned into a pigeon, not a bat, but it was better than nothing. He flapped his wings wildly, flailing and lurching after Odette.

"Vell, at least ve are rid of zose lunatics," Professor Von Skalpel said as he watched Snobula flap away. He closed the window.

"There you are," Odette said as Snobula flapped up to her. She had turned back into a human being and was

76

punching a number into her cell phone. "Otto, pick me up at the end of the road," she barked, then flipped the phone closed.

With a creak and a clack, Snobula turned back into his normal shape. His back was killing him.

"Vladdie, I'm proud of you," Odette said. "You showed them what you're made of. I know that everything will turn out all right for you."

"Thanks," Snobula said with a sigh. He pulled the chest from beneath his cape where he had hidden it, and held it out to Odette. "This is for you. The most worthy member of the family."

"Oh, pish-posh!" Odette said, waving her hand. Just then, the limousine pulled up, and the trunk popped open. Odette walked toward it. "I don't need the good-luck charm. It's yours. And the code—it's one thousand."

"One thousand?" Snobula repeated.

"Yep! See how easy that is to remember?" Odette asked. "Bye-bye! Come visit when you're traveling the world with all of your new riches!" Odette gave Snobula a kiss on the cheek, then climbed into her coffin.

Snobula hurried back to the Manor. The sun was about to rise, and he didn't want to be caught outside. He tiptoed into his room and double-locked the door. Then he pulled out

the chest and smiled at it.

"One thousand," Snobula murmured, staring at the numbers, which were at 000999. He laughed softly and turned the dials.

With a click, the lid opened.

Count Snobula's hand trembled as he lifted the lid. This was it. His chance to begin again! He would be rich! He would be powerful! He would have a shiny, new pair of shoes!

He reached into the box, wondering what the good-luck charm would be. A precious gem? A golden necklace? An ancient spell?

But it was simply a card marked with a question mark. There was something familiar about it. Count Snobula flipped it over.

Risk. Collect five hundred dollars from each player, the card read.

Snobula stared, then started to laugh. It was a Risk card from the Monstrosity game!

When his grandmother had told him to take a risk—she had meant a Risk card!

He had gone to all of that trouble for nothing more than a pile of Monstrosity money.

Sighing, Count Snobula started to put the card back into the chest. But suddenly, he was struck with an idea. Yes . . . all he had to do was to get the other monsters to play a round of Monstrosity. Then he could bet a few quarters here and there—and secretly pull out his card when the time was right.

Count Snobula smiled. So he wouldn't be rich. But at least he'd have enough change to do his laundry. Which was pretty necessary, after his adventure in the barrel of body parts. And maybe he could win his glow-in-the-dark pen back.

Perhaps the card really was a good-luck charm, after all.